# Ms.
# Leakey Is
# Freaky!

# Ms. Leakey Is Freaky!

Dan Gutman

Pictures by
Jim Paillot

**HARPER**

*An Imprint of* HarperCollins*Publishers*

## To Emma

Ms. Leakey Is Freaky!

Text copyright © 2011 by Dan Gutman

Illustrations copyright © 2011 by Jim Paillot

All rights reserved. Printed in the United States of America.

Library of Congress Cataloging-in-Publication Data

Gutman, Dan.

   Ms. Leakey is freaky! / Dan Gutman ; pictures by Jim Paillot. — 1st ed.

      p.    cm. — (My weird school daze ; #12)

   Summary: Ella Mentry School hires a health teacher who tries to force the students to eat healthy foods and exercise, whether they want to or not.

   ISBN 978-0-06-170403-1 (lib. bdg.) — ISBN 978-0-06-170402-4 (pbk. bdg.)

   [1. Schools—Fiction. 2. Health—Fiction. 3. Food habits—Fiction. 4. Exercise—Fiction. 5. Humorous stories.]   I. Paillot, Jim, ill.  II. Title.

PZ7.G9846Mwl 2011                           2010022975

[Fic]—dc22                                       CIP

                                                   AC

Typography by Joel Tippie

17    CG/RRDH    10  9  8  7  6  5

❖

First Edition

# Contents

# Health Nuts

My name is A.J. and I hate school.

I go to Ella Mentry School. It was named after an old lady named Ella Mentry.

Every time I tell somebody I go to Ella Mentry School, they always ask, "Which one?"

"I told you," I say. "Ella Mentry School."

"*Everybody* goes to elementary school," they always say.

"No they don't," I tell them.

"Yes they do."

See what I mean? If you ask me, it would have been a lot smarter if they named my school after somebody famous, like George Washington or Lady Gaga.

My teacher is Mr. Granite, who is from another planet. It was Monday morning. Mr. Granite said we had to go to an assembly.* I sat with my friends Michael, Ryan, and Neil, who we call the nude kid even though he wears clothes. In front of

---

* What's up with that? We never assemble anything. They should have assemblies with no assembly required.

us sat crybaby Emily and Andrea Young, this annoying girl with curly brown hair that I hate.

After we pledged the allegiance, our principal, Mr. Klutz, climbed up on the stage. He has no hair at all. Mr. Klutz used to have hair, but it fell out. That's what happens when guys get old. I wonder if he still has his hair in a plastic bag at home so he can look at it and remember what it was like to be young.

Everybody was talking. So Mr. Klutz made a peace sign with his fingers, which means "Shut up!" We all stopped talking.

"Kids today eat too much junk food," he told us. "Too much fat and too much sugar.

And you don't get enough exercise. That's why I hired Ms. Leakey, our new health teacher. She would like to say a few words."

Ms. Leakey came bounding up on the stage like she was in a race or something. We gave her a round of applause by clapping our hands in big circles. She was holding a garbage can cover in one hand and a sword in the other hand. That was weird.

"Thank you," Ms. Leakey said. "I'd like to introduce you to my best friends. I hope they'll become *your* best friends too."

Our media specialist, Mrs. Roopy, came out from behind the curtain. Only she wasn't dressed like a media specialist. She was wearing a big banana costume.

Then our reading specialist, Mr. Macky, came out. He was dressed up like a giant peanut.

Behind Mr. Macky was our school

nurse, Mrs. Cooney. She had on a carrot costume. And all three of them were holding swords. It was a real Kodak moment.

Suddenly, they all started singing . . .

*"Veggies are so good for you*
*Nuts have lots of protein.*
*Fruits are fun to peel and chew*
*Someday we'll join a pro team.*
*Drink your milk every day*
*Eat carrots for your eyes*
*Build strong bodies every way*
*And get lots of exercise!"*

While they were singing, our Spanish teacher, Miss Holly, our speech teacher,

Miss Laney, and our security guard, Officer Spence, came out from behind the curtain on the other side of the stage. They were dressed up like a candy bar, a can of soda, and a donut. And they all had swords.

"Check out those health nuts!" said Miss Holly.

"That song is really lame," said Miss Laney.

"Fruits and veggies are for *losers*!" said Officer Spence.

Ms. Leakey stopped singing and glared at the candy bar, can of soda, and donut.

"Hey, you bums!" she yelled. "We're trying to sing a song here. So get off the stage!"

"Who's gonna *make* us?" said Miss Holly.

"*Ooooooooooooooooohhhhh,*" all the kids in the audience went.

"*We're* going to make you!" said Ms. Leakey.

"*Ooooooooooooooooohhhhh,*" we all went.

At that moment, the weirdest thing in the history of the world happened. Ms. Leakey yelled, "Charge!"

And they all started fighting!

# Clash of the Titans

You should have been there! It was a wild scene on the stage. The banana was sword fighting with the candy bar! The peanut was sword fighting with the can of soda! The carrot was sword fighting with the donut! It was hilarious. And we got to see it live and in person.

"I'm full of protein!" shouted the peanut as he swung his sword around. "I have lots of energy!"

"Get lean and mean by eating greens!" shouted the carrot.

"I'm low in fat!" shouted the banana. "And a good source of fiber and vitamins!"

"I will make you fat and slow!" shouted

the candy bar as she charged with her sword.

"I will clog your arteries!" shouted the donut.

"I will ruin your appetite for dinner!" shouted the can of soda.

They were all running around the stage sword fighting with each other. It was like

*Clash of the Titans* but with food. The banana hit the candy bar over the head, and it toppled over.

"I fell down and I can't get up!" shouted the candy bar. "I'm too tired!"

In front of me, Andrea was talking to her crybaby friend, Emily.

"This skit is very violent," she said. "I'm not sure it's appropriate for children."

"Can you possibly be more boring?" I told her.

"Oh, snap!" said Ryan.

Except for Andrea and Emily, all the kids were yelling and screaming with excitement. Up on the stage, the peanut knocked the sword out of the soda can's hand. The soda can ran away. Everybody cheered. Ms. Leakey and the carrot were fighting with Officer Spence, I mean, the donut. It was awesome.

"I'm good for you!" shouted the carrot.

"But I taste better!" shouted the donut.

"Sugar and fat are my enemies!" shouted Ms. Leakey. "They must be your enemies too."

Ms. Leakey kept stabbing her sword at the donut, but Officer Spence was jumping around, so the sword only hit the donut hole. He was fighting back hard, but it was two against one. Ms. Leakey got on one side of him, and the carrot got on his other side.

"This is for your own good, donut!" shouted Ms. Leakey. "Charge!"

And then, together, they stabbed the donut!

"Die, empty calories!" Ms. Leakey shouted.

Officer Spence let out a scream, and then he fell to his donut knees and started crying.

When they pulled the swords out of him, chocolate syrup started squirting all over the place like a fountain. I thought I was gonna throw up, but it was cool.

"This is *really* inappropriate for children," said Andrea.

What is her problem? Andrea is no fun at all.

"Help!" shouted the donut. "I'm losing my partially hydrogenated corn syrup!"

"Victory is . . . sweet!" shouted Ms. Leakey.

"Oh, untimely death!" Officer Spence moaned. And then he fell forward and stopped moving.

Ms. Leakey, Mrs. Roopy, Mr. Macky, and

Mrs. Cooney went to the front of the stage and took a bow. We all clapped in a big circle.

"Thank you," Ms. Leakey said. "I hope you liked our performance. If you'll excuse me, I need to go do some push-ups."

Then she ran away. We all clapped again.

Mr. Klutz climbed up on the stage and made the shut up peace sign to calm everybody down.

"Well, that was exciting!" he said. "So, did you kids learn anything from this skit?"

"Yeah," I hollered. "Sword fighting is *cool*!"

# Girls Rule.
# Boys Drool.

The guys and I all agreed that sword fighting was cool. Instead of us playing games in fizz ed, they should let us fight with swords. All that running and jumping and stabbing each other would be good exercise.

After the assembly we went back to

Mr. Granite's class. It was time for math. I hate math.

"Let's say there are fifteen lightbulbs burning in your house," Mr. Granite told us, "and you turn off seven of them when you leave for school. How many are still burning?"

"Eight!" we all shouted.

"Wrong!" said Mr. Granite. "The correct answer is zero. You should never leave *any* lights burning when you leave your house. It's a waste of electricity."

That's when the most amazing thing in the history of the world happened. Ms. Leakey, the health teacher, came running into the room. That lady must run *everywhere*.

"To what do we owe the pleasure of your company?" asked Mr. Granite.

That's grown-up talk for "What are *you* doing here?"

"It's time for health class!" Ms. Leakey said, all excited. "Everybody up on your feet!"

"Uh, we're in the middle of a math lesson right now," said Mr. Granite.

"Great!" said Ms. Leakey. "The kids can count while they do jumping jacks! Let's go! One! Two! Three! Four!"

Mr. Granite didn't look very happy that his math lesson had been interrupted. He picked up a newspaper and started reading it. We all got up and started doing jumping jacks with Ms. Leakey. I don't really like to do jumping jacks, but it was better than doing math.

"Five! Six! Seven! Eight!" shouted Ms. Leakey. "Let's get that blood flowing!"

"Ew, disgusting!" I said as I jumped up and down. "I don't want my blood flowing."

"If your blood didn't flow, you would *die*, Arlo," said Andrea, who calls me by

my real name because she knows I don't like it.

"Your *face* should die," I told Andrea.

Ms. Leakey made us touch our toes, reach for the sky, bend over backward, and do all kinds of other weird stuff. Then she told us to sit down so she could talk about nutrition.

"Your body is like a machine," Ms. Leakey told us. "The heart is like the engine of your body, and the food you eat is like the battery. Candy, chips, cookies, and junk food make weak batteries. If you want strong batteries, you need to eat fruits and vegetables—things that grow out of the ground."

"Ew, I'm not gonna eat something that grew in *dirt*!" I said. "That's disgusting."

"Sugar grows in dirt," Ms. Leakey told me.

"That must be some *sweet* dirt," I said.

"Do you kids know which is the most important meal of the day?" asked Ms. Leakey.

Little Miss Perfect was waving her arm around like it was on fire. Naturally, Ms. Leakey called on her.

"Breakfast!" Andrea said, all proud of herself.

"That's right," Ms. Leakey said. "Breakfast is the most important meal of the day."

"Breakfast is conceited," I said. "Mr.

Granite told us you shouldn't think you're more important than anyone else."

I looked at Mr. Granite. He was in the back of the room reading his newspaper. He looked annoyed.

"Yeah," said Ryan. "How does that make lunch feel?"

"Do you think lunch and dinner are jealous of breakfast because it's more important?" asked Michael.

"Lunch and dinner don't have feelings," Ms. Leakey told us. "They're just *meals.*"

"Didn't we learn in social studies that all meals are created equal?" I asked.

"That's *men*, dumbhead!" said Andrea. "All *men* are created equal."

"Your *face* is a man," I told Andrea.

"That doesn't even make sense, Arlo!"

"Your *face* doesn't make sense," I told Andrea.

"Oh, snap!" said Ryan.

"I think breakfast is selfish," said Neil the nude kid.

"You eat shellfish for breakfast?" I asked. "That's weird."

"Can we get back on task, please?" said Ms. Leakey. "What I'm trying to say is that what you eat is very important. Don't you want to grow up to be strong like me?"

Ms. Leakey flexed her arm muscles like a bodybuilder.

"I'll bet you're not as strong as Mr.

Granite," said Ryan. "He's *really* strong."

"Oh, yeah? I'll bet I'm *stronger* than Mr. Granite!" said Ms. Leakey.

"*Ooooooooooooooohhhhh,*" we all went.

Mr. Granite looked up from his newspaper.

"Are you challenging me, Ms. Leakey?" he said.

"*Ooooooooooooooohhhhh,*" we all went.

"You wanna arm wrestle?" Ms. Leakey said.

"Bring it on!" said Mr. Granite.

"*Ooooooooooooooohhhhh,*" we all went.

Mr. Granite and Ms. Leakey went to Mr. Granite's desk and put their elbows next to each other. Ms. Leakey glared at Mr. Granite. Mr. Granite glared at Ms. Leakey. Then they gripped each other's hands and started arm wrestling.

"Go, Mr. Granite!" yelled all the boys.

"You can beat him, Ms. Leakey!" yelled all the girls.

Mr. Granite and Ms. Leakey were moaning and grunting while their arms moved left and right. There was sweat all over Mr. Granite's face. And soon Ms. Leakey's hand was pushing Mr. Granite's hand toward the desk. She slammed it down with a thud.

"Victory is sweet!" shouted Ms. Leakey.

"WOW," we all went, which is "MOM" upside down.

All the girls were yelling and screaming and hooting and hollering. All the boys were booing and saying Ms. Leakey cheated.

And you'll never believe who walked into the door at that moment.

Nobody. If you walked into a door it would hurt. But you'll never believe who walked into the *doorway*.

It was Mr. Klutz!

"What's going on in here?" he asked. "I heard yelling all the way down the hall."

"Ms. Leakey beat Mr. Granite at arm wrestling!" said Andrea.

"Well, I'll bet she can't beat *me* at arm wrestling!" said Mr. Klutz.

*"Oooooooooooooooohhhhh,"* we all went.

"I'll take that bet," said Ms. Leakey.

Mr. Klutz got into arm wrestling position with Ms. Leakey. They glared at each other.

"You're going *down*," said Mr. Klutz.

"I don't *think* so!" said Ms. Leakey.

That's when the yelling and screaming and grunting and sweating started. And when it was all over, Mr. Klutz was rubbing his arm in pain.

"Girls rule! Boys drool!" shouted the girls.

"Is there anyone else you'd like me to humiliate?" asked Ms. Leakey.

"Yes," said Mr. Klutz as he pulled out his walkie-talkie. "Officer Spence, will you please report to Mr. Granite's class?"

A few minutes later, Officer Spence arrived. He's a really big guy, and he's really strong.

"Is anything wrong?" asked Officer Spence.

"Yes," Mr. Klutz said. "Ms. Leakey beat me at arm wrestling. For the sake of all the men in the world, I need you to avenge my defeat."

"Sure thing, boss," said Officer Spence. "No man *or* woman can beat *me* at arm wrestling."

We were all yelling and screaming and freaking out as Ms. Leakey and Officer Spence started arm wrestling. First he almost pushed her hand all the way down to the desk. Then she almost pushed his hand all the way down to the desk. They went back and forth like that for a while.

And then, finally, Officer Spence was moaning and grunting as his hand moved backward. It looked like his eyes were going to pop out of his head.

And then he gave up, and his hand hit the desk.

"Yay!" shouted all the girls.

"Boo!" shouted all the boys.

"I think I proved my point," said Ms. Leakey. "If you eat your fruits and veggies and drink lots of milk, you'll get strong like me. Well, if you'll excuse me, I need to go do some sit-ups."

With that she ran away.

Ms. Leakey sure is strong. But she also sure is weird.

# The Perfect Food

Soon it was time for lunch in the vomitorium. Me and the guys sat at our usual table. Andrea and her girlie friends sat at the next table so they could bother us.

Michael had a ham sandwich. Ryan bought the school lunch, which is disgusting. He'll eat anything, even stuff that isn't food. My mom packed me a peanut butter sandwich and a Twinkie.

"Do you think we would *really* get strong if we ate more fruits and veggies?" asked Neil the nude kid.

"It would be cool to be strong like Ms. Leakey," said Michael. "Then we could sword fight with lots of bad guys dressed like food and beat everybody at arm wrestling."

"I ate a piece of asparagus once," I told the guys. "It was gross. I thought I was gonna die."

That's when Little Miss Know-It-All at the next table turned around.

"Ms. Leakey is right, you know," Andrea

said. "Eating healthy food is good for your body."

When Andrea turned back around, we all made faces at her.

"Ms. Leakey is weird," said Ryan. "Why do you think she's always running out of the room?"

"She needs to go exercise," said Michael. "She's obsessed with exercise."

I finished my sandwich and peeled the wrapper off my Twinkie. I don't know if you've ever eaten a Twinkie, but it is the best food in the history of the world. I could eat Twinkies all day long. Well, not in the shower. That would be weird. But Twinkies are the perfect food.

I was about to put the Twinkie in my mouth when the weirdest thing in the history of the world happened.

"STOP!" a voice shouted.

It was Ms. Leakey! She came running full speed into the vomitorium like she was in the Olympics. She appeared out of *nowhere*! She must have a Twinkie detector or something.

"DROP THAT TWINKIE!" Ms. Leakey screamed as she grabbed my hand.

The Twinkie was an inch from my mouth.

"But I'm hungry!" I complained.

"Do you know what that thing is made of?" asked Ms. Leakey.

"Uh, golden sponge cake with creamy filling?"

"No!" she shouted. "Dextrose! Sodium acid pyrophosphate! Diglycerides! Polysorbate 60! Partially hydrogenated animal shortening! You want to put all those chemicals into your body?"

The Twinkie was still an inch from my mouth. I looked at it. Then I looked at Ms. Leakey. Then I looked at the Twinkie again. Then I looked at Ms. Leakey again.

"Eat it, A.J.," whispered Ryan. "She can't tell you what to do."

"Don't eat it, A.J.," said Michael.

"Eat it, A.J.," whispered Neil the nude kid.

"Don't eat it, Arlo," said Andrea.

I was faced with the hardest decision of my life. I didn't know what to do. I didn't know what to say. I had to think fast. I was concentrating so hard that my brain hurt.

And then I leaned forward and took a bite of the Twinkie. Ms. Leakey grabbed my upper and lower teeth with her hands and tried to pull them apart.

"Spit out the Twinkie, A.J.!" she screamed. "Stop this junk food madness!"

"But I *love* sodium acid pyrophosphate!" I yelled.

I managed to swallow that bite of Twinkie, but Ms. Leakey grabbed the

rest of it out of my lunch box. Then she
jumped up on top of our table.

"Do you kids know that the average

person eats fifty pounds of cookies and cake every year?" she shouted so everybody in the vomitorium could hear. "You eat eighteen pounds of candy! Five pounds of potato chips! A hundred pounds of sugar! No wonder today's kids are so unhealthy!"

Ms. Leakey jumped down from the table and grabbed one of the big garbage cans we scrape our trays into. Then she started taking Ding Dongs and Yodels and cupcakes off kids' trays and throwing them into the garbage can.

"Free yourselves from the shackles of sugar!" she shouted. "Put your junk food in here! Begin a new life for yourself! Join the sugar-free revolution!"

Some of the kids actually threw their junk food into the garbage can. What is their problem?

"Come, follow me, everyone!" Ms. Leakey yelled, pulling the garbage can behind her. She marched out the door of the vomitorium and started singing . . .

*"Drink your milk every day*
*Eat carrots for your eyes*
*Build strong bodies every way*
*And get lots of exercise!"*

Everybody followed Ms. Leakey out the door. She dragged the garbage can across the playground to the corner. There's a big, green Dumpster there.

"This is where junk food belongs!" shouted Ms. Leakey. She picked the garbage can up over her head with super-human strength and emptied it into the Dumpster.

"Throw it away! Throw it away!" kids were chanting.

It was horrible! What a waste of perfectly good junk food.

This was worse than TV Turnoff Week. It was the worst day of my life.

# Being Frank

After lunch we went back to Mr. Granite's class. He was talking about recycling paper when the school secretary, Mrs. Patty, made an announcement over the loudspeaker.

"Mr. Granite, please send A.J. to Ms. Leakey's office."

"*Oooooooooooh*, A.J.'s in trouble!" said Ryan.

"I told you not to eat that Twinkie, dude," said Michael.

"Maybe Arlo will get kicked out of school!" said Andrea.

She was rubbing her hands together. That's what people do when they want something really badly. Why can't a truck full of Twinkies fall on Andrea's head?

I didn't want to go to Ms. Leakey's office. You know where I wanted to go? Antarctica. I wanted to run away and live with the penguins. Penguins are cool. Nobody tells penguins they can't eat Twinkies.

I walked really slowly down the hall.*
When I opened the door to Ms. Leakey's office, she wasn't in there. I looked
around. It was a weird office. There was a
treadmill, an organ, a bunch of plants, a
giant metal box that looked like a coffin,
a hot tub, and a punching bag hanging
from the ceiling!

---

* My friend Billy, who lives around the corner, told me that
if you walk backward really fast, you can travel through
time. I tried to do that once, but I smashed into a tree.

Suddenly, the strangest thing in the history of the world happened. That giant box opened up, and a monster popped out!

*"Aaaaaaaaaaaaaaaahhhhh!"* I screamed.

The monster pulled a mask off its face.

It wasn't a monster after all. It was Ms. Leakey!

"Hi, A.J.!" she said.

"Why were you lying in a metal box with a mask on your face?" I asked.

"Oh, this is my hyperbaric chamber," she said. "I was breathing pure oxygen. It's good for the lungs."

"A hyper-what?" I asked. "Where do you get one of those things?"

"From Rent-A-Hyperbaric Chamber," she said. "You can rent anything."

I looked at the row of plants under the window.

"Why do you have a farm in your office?" I asked.

"I grow all my own food," she told me. "It's organic."

I guess that means she plays the organ while her food grows. That's weird.

"What's with the hot tub?" I asked.

"It's not a hot tub," Ms. Leakey told me. "It's an endless pool. I swim laps in it."

"Really short laps, huh?" I said.

"The endless pool has a current, like a river," Ms. Leakey told me. "The water shoots past you so you swim in one place. You can swim forever."

That made no sense at all. Who wants to swim forever without going anywhere?

Ms. Leakey got up out of her weird box.

"Would you like some trail mix, A.J.?" she said, holding out a bag to me.

I looked inside the bag. The stuff looked gross.

"No thanks," I said. "I don't want to eat trail."

"It's nuts and fruits and berries," said Ms. Leakey. "All natural things. Trail mix is good for you."

"That's why I don't want to eat it."

"A.J.," Ms. Leakey said, "can I be frank with you?"

"You can call yourself whatever you want, Frank," I told her.

"I'm concerned about your diet," she said. "Tell me, are you getting three square meals a day at home?"

"Well, sometimes my meals are round, Frank," I told her. "Like when we have pizza, or pancakes."

Ms. Leakey just shook her head sadly.

"Why do you have a punching bag in

here?" I asked her.

"Eating junk food makes kids frustrated," she told me. "It helps if they punch the bag. It's good exercise, too."

"Hitting stuff is fun," I agreed.

"Would you like to try it, A.J.?"

"Sure."

Ms. Leakey got a pair of boxing gloves from her closet and put them on me.

"Okay, hit that bag, A.J.!" she said.

I hit the bag. It felt good.

"Hit it again, A.J." Ms. Leakey yelled. "Harder!"

I punched the bag some more, as hard as I could.

"Punch out fat, A.J.!" shouted Ms.

Leakey. "Punch out sugar!"

I started dancing around the bag like a boxer, punching it, kicking it, ramming it, slamming it. It was fun! That's when the weirdest thing in the history of the world happened.

A hole opened up in the punching bag. And you'll never believe in a million hundred years what fell out of the hole.

I'm not gonna tell you.

Okay, okay, I'll tell you.

It was candy! Candy and cookies and popcorn and all kinds of treats fell out! The punching bag was like a big piñata!

This was the greatest day of my life! I got down on my knees and started scooping up the candy. But I couldn't pick it up because of the boxing gloves.

"STOP!" Ms. Leakey shouted. "That candy isn't for eating! It's for punching!"

"But I want to eat it!" I begged. "I *love* candy!"

Ms. Leakey took the boxing gloves off me and walked me back down the hallway.

"A.J.," she said when we got to Mr. Granite's room, "you are going to be my special project this year. You're a student leader. The other kids want to do what you do. If I can get *you* to eat healthy, I think everyone else will follow. Will you at least *try* to eat better?"

"Okay," I said. "I'll try."

"Good," she replied. "I'll be keeping a very close eye on you to make sure you do. Now, if you'll excuse me, I need to go do my crunches."

"You're going to eat breakfast cereal, Frank?" I called after her.

But she didn't hear me. She had already run away.

# Meet Mr. Slug

The next day was Friday. After we pledged the allegiance, it was time for science class. Our science teacher is Mr. Docker. He has a car that runs on potatoes. Mr. Docker is off his rocker.

When we got to the science room, Mr. Docker was talking to a guy I never saw before.

"I'd like you to meet Mr. Harrison," Mr. Docker told us. "He's the new tech guy for our school."

"Tech guy?" we all asked. "What's a tech guy?"

"I fix things that are broken," said Mr. Harrison. "Computers, copy machines, telephones. I build things, too."

Mr. Harrison was tall and skinny. He had weird hair and one of those plastic pocket protectors on his shirt with a bunch of pens sticking out of it. His pants were too short. What a nerd!

"Mr. Harrison and I built something together," said Mr. Docker.

Mr. Harrison took a remote control out of his pocket and pushed a button. And you'll never believe what happened next. A robot came walking out of the closet!

"We want to introduce you to Mr. Slug," said Mr. Docker.

Mr. Slug walked to the front of the class, bumping into a few desks along the way. He didn't look like any robot I ever saw. He had a cigarette hanging out of his mouth, a can of beer in one hand, and a bag of potato chips in his other hand. His eyes were crossed. Mr. Slug was a mess.

"You shouldn't have cigarettes and beer in school," said Andrea. "It's a bad influence on children."

"Yes, we know," said Mr. Docker. "Ms. Leakey inspired us to build Mr. Slug. We wanted to show what happens to people who smoke and drink and eat poorly."

"Does Mr. Slug talk?" I asked.

"Sure," said Mr. Harrison. "Mr. Slug, how . . . are . . . you . . . feeling . . . today?"

Mr. Slug had a speaker on the side of his head. He made a sound like a cough. Then he coughed again. Then he had a coughing fit.

"OH . . . I . . . FEEL . . . LOUSY," Mr. Slug said in a computery voice. "I . . . AM . . . SO . . . TIRED. NEED . . . TO . . . LIE . . . DOWN. WHAT . . . DAY . . . IS . . . IT?"

Mr. Slug stumbled around the front of the room. Then he let out a burp.

"He doesn't sound very good," I said. "He sounds like he's gonna die."

"Does Mr. Slug run on batteries?" asked Michael.

"No," said Mr. Docker. "He runs on potatoes."

That figured.

"Check this out," said Mr. Harrison.

He opened a door in Mr. Slug's chest. You could look right into his body and see his insides. It was cool.

"Here's Mr. Slug's heart," said Mr. Harrison, "and here are his lungs. See how black they are? That's what happens when you smoke cigarettes."

Mr. Slug stumbled around the front of the room some more and then bumped into the whiteboard.

"OH . . . MY . . . HEAD." Mr. Slug moaned.

"So," said Mr. Docker. "Did you kids learn anything from Mr. Slug?"

"Yeah," I said, "robots are cool!"

# Fast Food

When I came home from school on Friday, my mom dumped the stuff from my backpack on the kitchen table like always. A piece of paper flew out. . . .

Come to the grand opening of . . .

# McLeakey's

Fast, healthy food for fast, healthy lives!

$10 off with this coupon

And kids eat FREE!

"Ms. Leakey must have opened her own restaurant," my mom said. "We should go there for dinner tonight."

"What kind of a restaurant is it?" I asked suspiciously.

"The coupon says it's fast food," my mom said.

Fast food? I *love* fast food!

When my dad came home from work, we all piled into the car to go to Ms. Leakey's new restaurant. There was a big sign out front:

# McLeakey's

My dad pulled the car up to the drive-through window.* There was a big clown face with a hole where his mouth should be next to the window.

"May I take your order?" asked the clown face.

"Tell the clown what you want, A.J.," said my dad.

"I'll have a hamburger," I said.

"You should avoid eating too much red

---

* What a dumb name. If you drove through a window, it would break. You'd probably get cut by the glass, too.

meat," the clown face said. "It has a lot of fat in it."

"Can I get a hot dog?" I asked.

"Are you crazy?" said the clown face. "Do you have any idea what they put in hot dogs? Trust me, you don't want to know."

"How about some chicken nuggets?" I asked.

"Don't even *think* about it!" said the clown face.

I slapped my head and looked in the window to check out the menu. It was hard to read the letters. I noticed there was a tree in the middle of the restaurant. That was weird.

"Well, what *do* you have?" I asked.

"We have broccoli burgers, meatless meatballs, vegetarian ribs, McMelon, ten kinds of tofu. . . ."

"Toe food!" I said. "I'm not eating food made from toes."

"Well, one of the kinds of tofu is nofu," said the clown face.

"What's that?" my dad asked.

"That's tofu with no toes in it," said the clown face.

"What do you have to drink?" I asked.

"Protein shakes, soy shakes, vitamin shakes, wheat grass shakes . . ."

"Can I just get a soda?" I asked.

"Are you out of your mind?" asked the clown face. "That stuff'll kill ya! One can of soda contains ten packets of sugar in it. You might as well just eat poison. How about a bowl of steam? It's ninety-nine cents."

"No thanks," I said. "I'm not hungry."

"Me neither," said my sister, Amy.

"Oh, and we have apples, too," said the clown face.

"We'll just have two apples," said my dad.

"Coming right up," said the clown face. "That will be one dollar. Pull up to the next window."

My dad drove up to the next window. There was a guy wearing a paper hat. My dad gave him a dollar bill. The guy reached behind him and pulled two apples off the tree that was in the middle of the restaurant. He tossed them to my dad.

"See, I told you it was fast food," said my mom.

McLeakey's is the weirdest restaurant in the history of the world.

# Sweets
# for the Sweet

My mom always goes grocery shopping on Saturday. And she always tries to get me to come along.

"A.J., let's go grocery shopping," she said.

"No thanks."

"Come on, A.J.," she said. "I'll let you push the cart."

"Oh, man, I want to watch TV, Mom."

"I'll buy you a treat," my mom said. "Sweets for the sweet!"

A treat! The last time I tasted anything sweet, it was that Twinkie that Ms. Leakey tried to grab out of my mouth. I hadn't had candy or cookies in so long, I hardly remembered what they tasted like.

"Let's go!" I told my mom.

We drove to the supermarket. My mom parked the car and got out her shopping list and coupons. I went to get a cart and pushed it through the magic doors that open all by themselves. Those doors are cool.

"Can I get my treat now, Mom?" I asked.

"Not yet," she told me. "First we have

to do our shopping."

Bummer in the summer! Shopping is way overrated. I don't know if you ever went grocery shopping with your mom or dad, but it is the most boring thing in the history of the world. We had to go up and down every aisle of the supermarket. I thought I was gonna die. All I wanted was my treat.

When my mom buys a melon, she acts like she's buying a house. She has to feel each melon. She has to smell each melon. Then she has to shake each melon and listen to it. What is her problem?

"It's just a *melon*!" I said. "They're all the same."

"I have to find the *perfect* melon," she said.

I hate melon.

Finally, after a million hundred hours, she found the perfect melon. We were finished grocery shopping.

"So, what treat do you want, A.J.?" my mom asked.

I had been thinking about it the whole time we were shopping. At first I wanted an ice-cream pop. But I decided that an ice-cream pop wouldn't last very long. Then I wanted a Devil Dog. But they come in boxes of eight, and I knew my mom would say I could only get *one* treat.

Then I saw something at the end of the

candy aisle. It was a giant box filled to the brim with candy. Just about every kind of candy in the world was in there. I led my mom over to it.

"Okay, you can have *one* treat, A.J.," my mom said. "Just one. I'll get in line. You choose your treat and meet me in the checkout line."

I looked over the candy: Milky Way, AirHeads, Mars bars, Twix, Kit Kat, Chunky, mr. Goodbar, York Peppermint Patties, Reese's Peanut Butter Cups, Mike and Ike, Atomic FireBall, JuJu Fish, Sour Neon Worms, Goobers, Laffy Taffy, Nerds, Sugar Daddy, Baby Ruth, Snickers, Kisses, M & M's (plain *and* peanut), gummi bears,

Dots, Junior Mints, Milk Duds, Good & Plenty, Whoppers, Twizzlers, Dum Dum, Skittles, Butterfinger, Starburst, Crunch, Jolly Rancher, Sweet Pops, Tootsie Roll. . . .

I couldn't decide which one I wanted. Everything looked so good. I wanted them *all*. I thought and thought and thought until my brain was about to explode. Finally, I decided to get a 3 Musketeers bar.

I leaned all the way over.

I reached out to pick up the 3 Musketeers bar.

I picked up the 3 Musketeers bar.

And you'll never believe in a million hundred years what happened next.

A hand came out from under all that candy! It grabbed *my* hand!

*"Aaaaaaaaaahhhhhhhhh!"* I screamed.

It was the scariest thing I had ever seen in my life! It was like one of those movies

where a zombie hand pops out of a grave in the middle of the night.

But then something even *scarier* happened. A person was attached to the hand! The person came up from under the candy.

And that person was . . . Ms. Leakey!

*"Aaaaaaaaaahhhhhhhhh!"* I screamed.

"DROP THAT CANDY BAR, A.J.!" Ms. Leakey said.

I dropped the 3 Musketeers bar. She was still holding my hand.

"What are you doing here?" I asked.

"Saving your life!" she said. "Do you know what they put in a 3 Musketeers bar? Hydrogenated palm kernel! Soy lecithin!

Corn syrup! Artificial flavors!"

Finally, she let go of my hand, and I ran all the way to the checkout line to meet my mom.

"So, which treat did you choose?" she asked me.

"I changed my mind," I told her. "I don't want a treat."

# 9

# Ms. Leakey Is Everywhere!

That night I was lying in bed. It was hard to fall asleep. All I could do was think about candy, cookies, cakes, ice cream, and junk food. I just wanted to taste something sweet again.

Then, suddenly, a lightbulb appeared

over my head.* I remembered something. A few months back, on Halloween, I'd taken a Hershey bar out of my Halloween candy and hidden it in my closet. I'd known there would come a day when I would want candy after Halloween was over. I had forgotten about it all this time.

The Hershey bar was still in my closet! I could eat it *now*! This was the greatest night of my life!

I got out of bed and opened my closet door. There's a lot of junk in there, but finally I found the Hershey bar.

I climbed back into bed with the Hershey bar.

---

* Well, not a *real* lightbulb. That would have been weird.

I unwrapped the Hershey bar.

*Ummm.* It smelled good.

I was about to take a bite of the Hershey bar when the weirdest thing in the history of the world happened.

Ms. Leakey jumped out from under my bed!

*"Aaaaaaaaaahhhhhhhhh!"* I screamed.

"DROP THAT HERSHEY BAR, A.J.!" Ms. Leakey said.

I dropped the Hershey bar. She picked it up.

"Why are you hiding under my bed?" I asked her. "How did you get in here?"

"I climbed in the window," she told me. "Do you know the average person eats

twenty-two pounds of candy every year?"

"But I just . . ."

"Well, if you'll excuse me," Ms. Leakey said, "I need to go do some squat thrusts."

I had no idea what a squat thrust was,

but it didn't matter. Ms. Leakey opened my window and climbed out. She was gone.

I was still sitting up in bed when my door opened. It was Mom and Dad.

"A.J., are you okay?" Mom asked.

"We heard a scream," said Dad.

"Ms. Leakey was here!" I told them. "She was hiding under my bed! I went to eat a Hershey bar, but she grabbed it out of my hand! And then she ran away!"

"There, there," my mom told me as she stroked my head. "You were just having a bad dream. Everything's fine, A.J."

"See?" my dad said. "Ms. Leakey isn't under your bed. It was just a nightmare."

"No, she was really here!" I insisted. "She

ran away! She climbed out the window!"

"*Sure* she did," Dad said.

"You go back to sleep, A.J." said my mom.

"In the morning you probably won't even

remember that this happened."

Oh, I'll remember. I know what I saw. Ms. Leakey was hiding under my bed, just like she was hiding under the candy in the supermarket.

She was following me! She was watching my every move to make sure I didn't eat candy, cookies, or junk food. She probably put a GPS in my brain so she could track me.

Ms. Leakey was *everywhere*.

# Junk Food Junkies

Ella Mentry School was getting healthy. *Disgustingly* healthy!

Every day, Mr. Granite told us we were more alert in class, we were standing up straighter, and we were full of energy.

There were no more soda machines in the school. No candy was allowed. Our lunch lady, Ms. LaGrange, was preparing healthy meals. Our moms and dads were packing lunches for us that were filled with fruits, nuts, vegetables, and other yucky stuff. Our custodian, Miss Lazar, put a sign in front of the school that said **SUGAR–FREE ZONE**. You weren't even allowed to have your parents bring in

cupcakes on your birthday anymore.

It was horrible!

"These tofu hot dogs are delicious!" said Little Miss Perfect while we were eating lunch in the vomitorium. "I feel so much healthier since Ms. Leakey arrived."

"Me too," said Emily, who always agrees with everything Andrea says.

"I wish I had a candy bar," said Michael.

"I heard Ms. Leakey is trying to pass a law that will make it illegal to be caught with sugar packets," said Ryan.

"I heard she hijacked a truck full of Doritos so it couldn't come into town," I said.

"Health teachers can't do that," said Neil the nude kid. "People should be allowed to make up their own minds about what to eat."

"Yeah!"

"Y'know, maybe Ms. Leakey isn't a health teacher at all," I said. "Did you ever think of that?"

"What do you mean?" asked Ryan.

"Maybe Ms. Leakey murdered our real

health teacher," I told them.

"Arlo, stop trying to scare Emily," said Andrea.

"I'm scared!" said Emily.

"Ms. Leakey is probably the evil twin of our real health teacher," I said. "She killed her sister, and I bet she buried her in the farm she's got in her office. Stuff like that happens all the time, you know."

"We've got to *do* something!" shouted Emily. And then she went running out of the vomitorium.

Sheesh, get a grip! That girl will fall for anything.

"I need candy," said Michael.

"I would pay a million dollars for a Kit

Kat right now," I said.

"I would sell my little brother for just one gummi bear," said Neil.

We were all candy deprived and depressed. But that's when I got the greatest idea in the history of the world.

"Hey!" I said. "I know where we can get some candy!"

"Where?" asked Ryan.

"Follow me."

I scraped off my tray into the garbage can. Then I led the guys out the door into the playground. Even Andrea came along.

It was recess, and kids were all over the playground. I led the gang over to the corner where the Dumpster is kept.

"That's where Ms. Leakey has been throwing our junk food," I said, pointing at the Dumpster.

"Of course!" said Ryan. "There must be *lots* of candy in there!"

"You're a genius, A.J.!" said Michael. "You should get the No Bell Prize."

"I don't know why we didn't think of this before!" said Neil the nude kid. "Dumpster diving is fun."

"I'm not eating candy out of a Dumpster," said Andrea. "It's dirty."

"Fine. Don't," I told her. "That will leave more for us. Let's go, guys!"

We sneaked around to the back of the

Dumpster really quietly, like secret agents.
It was cool.

"Don't do this, Arlo," whispered Andrea.

*"Shhhhh!"* I said. "If Ms. Leakey finds

us back here, we'll be in big trouble."

The Dumpster had a heavy lid on it. I couldn't lift it by myself.

Me and the guys put our hands on the edge of the lid.

We pushed open the lid.

And you'll never believe in a million hundred years what we saw in there.

I'm not gonna tell you.

Okay, okay, I'll tell you.

It was Ms. Leakey!

She was sitting on the bottom of the Dumpster, and she was surrounded by every kind of candy and junk food in the world! There were AirHeads, Mars bars, Reese's Pieces, Atomic FireBalls, Goobers,

Nerds, Dots, Milk Duds, Whoppers, Twiz-zlers, Skittles, Tootsie Rolls. . . .

Well, you get the idea.

And you know what Ms. Leakey had in her mouth?

A Twinkie!

"Ms. Leakey!" I shouted. "What are *you* doing in here?"

Her mouth was full of sodium acid pyrophosphate and all those other chemi-cals, so she couldn't answer right away.

"I'm . . . guarding the Dumpster," Ms. Leakey finally said, "to make sure nobody eats this horrible junk food."

"You're eating a Twinkie!" I said.

"No, I'm not. I'm . . . conducting an

experiment," she said, "I want to see if any of the chemicals in a Twinkie can be used to solve the energy problem. Maybe someday we will have cars that run on Twinkies. This is research."

"It is not!" shouted Andrea. "You're stuffing your face with junk food! You're a hypocrite!"

"A what?" I said. "She doesn't look like a hippo to me."

"Not a hippo, dumbhead," Andrea said. "A hypocrite. That's somebody who acts like they're better than everyone, but they're really worse."

"It's true! It's true!" Ms. Leakey said, sobbing. "I admit it. I'm not a health nut.

I need sugar! I need sweets! I need candy! I'm a junk food junkie!"

And then she scooped up a handful of candy, jumped out of the Dumpster, and ran away.

Ms. Leakey is freaky!

# The New Health Teacher

Well, word got around pretty fast that Ms. Leakey was stuffing her face with junk food. Everybody was wondering if she would come to school the next day. And sure enough, she was nowhere to be found. We even looked in the Dumpster.

Me and the guys went to Mr. Klutz's

office to find out what happened.

"Where's Ms. Leakey?" I asked.

"I fired her," Mr. Klutz said. "You know how she was always running away to go exercise? Well, it turned out that she was just running to the Dumpster to eat junk food."

"So you fired her just because she ate junk food?" Ryan asked.

"No," Mr. Klutz said,

"I fired her because she went overboard."

"She fell out of a boat?" I asked.*

"No, no," Mr. Klutz told me. "Ms. Leakey just went too far with all that health food stuff. I think it's okay to have junk food once in a while, as a treat. You just have to be careful not to overdo it."

"So I guess we don't have a health teacher anymore," Michael said.

"Sure we do," said Mr. Klutz. "Let me introduce you to our *new* health teacher."

He took a remote control out of his pocket and pushed a button. And you'll never believe who walked into the door at that moment.

---

* Why are people always talking about boats?

It was Mr. Slug! He actually walked right into the door!

"OUCH!" said Mr. Slug. "I . . . HIT . . . MY . . . HEAD . . . ON . . . THE . . . DOOR."

"Mr. Slug is our new health teacher?" I asked. "He doesn't know *anything* about health."

"Sure he does," Mr. Klutz said. "He'll show you what you shouldn't do if you want to be healthy."

"I . . . FEEL . . . LOUSY . . . ," said Mr. Slug. "NEED . . . TO . . . LIE . . . DOWN."

"Maybe you should go outside and get some exercise," Ryan suggested. "Then you'll feel better."

"OUTSIDE?" said Mr. Slug. "ARE . . .

YOU . . . CRAZY? YOU . . . COULD . . .
GET . . . HIT . . . BY . . . A . . . BUS . . . OUT . . .
THERE. EXERCISING . . . IS . . . DANGER-
OUS. LET'S . . . JUST . . . CHILL . . . IN . . .
HERE . . . WHERE . . . IT . . . IS . . . SAFE."

"Is it okay if we go eat some of the junk
food in the Dumpster?" I asked.

"WHATEVER," said Mr. Slug.

* * *

Well, that's pretty much the way it happened. Maybe Ms. Leakey will stop hiding under my bed and stalking me in supermarkets. Maybe the police will find Ms. Leakey's twin sister buried in the farm in her office. Maybe McLeakey's restaurant will get some food people want to eat. Maybe my mom will start making square pizzas. Maybe I'll go to Antarctica and eat Twinkies with the penguins. Maybe I'll try asparagus again. Maybe Mr. Slug will quit smoking and stop walking into doors. Maybe the teachers will stop arm wrestling with each other. Maybe breakfast will stop thinking it's so important. Maybe they'll let us do sword fighting in fizz ed. Maybe our teachers will stop dressing up like food. Maybe people will stop talking about boats all the time. Maybe Mr. Klutz will show us his plastic bag full of hair. Maybe I'll find the GPS that Ms. Leakey put in my brain.

But it won't be easy!